The Scaredy Cat

Swim into more

PuRRMaiDS

adventures!

The Scaredy Cat
The Catfish Club
Seasick Sea Horse

Bardhan-Quallen, Sudipta.,author
Scaredy cat

2017
33305247473873
ca   12/31/19

The Scaredy Cat

by Sudipta Bardhan-Quallen

illustrations by Vivien Wu

A STEPPING STONE BOOK™
Random House 🏠 New York

This is a work of fiction. Names, characters, places, and incidents either are the product of the author's imagination or are used fictitiously. Any resemblance to actual persons, living or dead, events, or locales is entirely coincidental.

Text copyright © 2017 by Sudipta Bardhan-Quallen
Cover art copyright © 2017 by Andrew Farley
Interior illustrations copyright © 2017 by Vivien Wu

All rights reserved. Published in the United States by Random House Children's Books, a division of Penguin Random House LLC, New York.

Random House and the colophon are registered trademarks and A Stepping Stone Book and the colophon are trademarks of Penguin Random House LLC. PURRMAIDS® is a registered trademark of KIKIDOODLE LLC and is used under license from KIKIDOODLE LLC.

Visit us on the Web!
randomhousekids.com
SteppingStonesBooks.com

Educators and librarians, for a variety of teaching tools, visit us at
RHTeachersLibrarians.com

Library of Congress Cataloging-in-Publication Data is available upon request.
ISBN 978-1-5247-0161-1 (trade) — ISBN 978-1-5247-0162-8 (lib. bdg.)
ISBN 978-1-5247-0163-5 (ebook)

Printed in the United States of America
10 9 8
First Edition

This book has been officially leveled by using the F&P Text Level Gradient™ Leveling System.

Random House Children's Books supports the
First Amendment and celebrates the right to read.

To Rachel, who always helps me create beautiful
things from interesting combinations

It was a paw-sitively beautiful morning in Kittentail Cove. Coral was very excited. After waiting all summer, it was finally the first day of sea school!

Coral carefully brushed her orange fur. She chose a sparkly headband to wear. Then she snapped a bracelet on her paw. It was her favorite because of the golden seashell charm. It matched the ones Angel and Shelly had.

Angel, Shelly, and Coral had been friends fur-ever. They met when they were tiny kittens. On the outside, they looked very different. They often had different ideas about what to do, where to go, and how much trouble they should get into. But somehow their differences made them purr-fect partners. Coral couldn't imagine being without Angel and Shelly.

In fact, one of her favorite things about school was that she got to be with her best friends all day.

Coral grabbed her bag and went to the door. "Bye, Papa! Bye, Mama!" she called. "See you later!"

"Good luck, Coral," Papa answered. "Don't

forget that you, Angel, and Shelly are coming here after school."

"I know, Papa," Coral replied. With a wave goodbye, she swam off. She was meeting Angel and Shelly in Leondra's Square, under the statue of Leondra, the founder of Kittentail Cove.

Purrmaids lived in every part of every ocean. They had towns in coves, reefs, and anywhere else that was beautiful and peaceful. Kittentail Cove was the best purrmaid town in the world! At least, Coral thought so.

"I hope Angel and Shelly are there already!" Coral purred. Shelly was usually on time, but Angel often ran late. The sooner they met up, the sooner they'd get to school to meet their new teacher. Coral was excited to see who it would be.

Besides, the first day of school was a terrible time to be late!

As she swam toward the statue, Coral saw Shelly. Even from far away, Shelly looked lovely. Every strand of her white fur was purr-fectly in place. She had a small starfish clip near her ear, and the golden seashell charm on her bracelet glittered.

"Shelly!" Coral called. "Have you seen Angel?"

Shelly looked up and waved to Coral. She started to say, "No, I haven't—"

"I'm right here!" someone shouted.

It was Angel! Coral spun around to face her friend.

Like Coral and Shelly, Angel was dressed up for the first day of school. She was wearing a necklace of red starfish. The red looked beautiful against her black-and-white fur. And just like her best friends, Angel wore her golden seashell bracelet.

"What are you two waiting for?" Angel asked as she swam past her friends. "We have to swim to school!"

Coral bit back a smile. "You were late— and now you're telling *us* to hurry?"

Shelly laughed. "We'd better catch up. We don't want to miss the bell!"

When the girls arrived at sea school, Angel groaned. "Coral! We're early! No one else is even here yet!"

Coral giggled. "It's better to be early than late."

"But I could have slept longer!" Angel whined.

Shelly patted Angel's paw. "Since we're here, let's find our classroom," she suggested.

Angel scowled for a moment. But then she nodded. "Room Sea-Seven, right?" she asked.

"No, silly." Coral laughed. "That was our classroom *last* year!"

"We're in Eel-Twelve this year," Shelly added.

They made their way toward Eel-Twelve. There was a purrmaid inside the classroom when they arrived. She didn't look like most of the purrmaids in town. Her long fur was dyed every color of the rainbow. She wore three earrings on her left ear and four on her right. Even her tail was decorated with shiny rings!

"Is that our *teacher*?" Angel whispered.

"I think so," Coral answered.

"I've never seen a teacher who looks like that," Shelly said. "She's so cool!"

"Let's go meet her!" Angel suggested.

The girls swam into the classroom. The colorful purrmaid had her back to the door, but she spun around as the girls entered. "I thought I heard some curious little kittens," she said. "You're here early. You must love school!"

"We do!" said all three friends at once.

Their teacher grinned. "I'm glad to hear that. I'm Ms. Harbor, and today is my first day, too."

"I'm Coral," said Coral, "and these are my friends, Angel and Shelly."

"It's lovely to meet you all," Ms. Harbor purred.

The bell rang, so the purrmaids swam to their clamshell seats. Ms. Harbor welcomed more students into the classroom. Then she swam to her giant scallop-shell teacher's chair. "Let's begin, class!" she said.

There was so much to do on the first day of school that Coral lost track of time. She was surprised when Ms. Harbor announced, "Our first day is almost over, but I have some homework for you tonight."

All the students groaned. "Homework!" Angel said. "Already?"

Ms. Harbor held her paws up for silence. "This homework isn't hard, I purr-omise. In fact, you might enjoy it." She floated to the middle of the classroom. "I want to tell you something about me. I love curiosity! Curious purrmaids are not afraid to learn. That's how you find the most interesting things in the ocean!"

Coral nodded. She loved exploring the ocean, too—as long as the exploring part wasn't too scary.

"I am very excited to be your teacher this year," Ms. Harbor continued. "We are going to have a fin-tastic time learning from each other and making waves in Kittentail Cove! To start our year, I'd like each of you to bring something special to class tomorrow."

"What do you mean by 'special'?" Angel asked.

"It can be anything you want!" Ms. Harbor laughed. "Your favorite shell, a beautiful pearl, a pet sea horse. Whatever will show me how you see life's beauty. Help me learn about you!"

2

Coral always felt like she had to swim twice as fast to keep up with Angel and Shelly. But on the way home from school, it was a lot harder than usual. Angel zipped through the streets toward Coral's house so quickly that even Shelly fell behind.

"Slow down, Angel!" Shelly shouted. But Angel didn't stop.

"Don't even try," Coral said. "Angel is excited about something. And when she's excited, nothing makes her slow down!"

"What do you think is going on?" Shelly asked.

Coral shrugged. "I don't know. But I bet it has to do with our homework."

Angel didn't wait for Coral to finish hugging Mama before she asked a question. "What are you two going to do about the homework assignment?"

"Hello to you, too, Angel," Mama said.

Angel mumbled, "Hello, Mrs. Marsh."

Mama smiled. "The first day of school must have gone really well if you are this excited about homework!"

"It did!" the friends answered at the same time.

"I'm glad," Mama said. "Have fun doing your homework."

Coral kissed Mama's cheek. Then she waved for her friends to follow her to her bedroom. "This is what I'm going to bring," she announced. She held up a pink pointy turret shell. "This one is my favorite."

"It's beautiful," Shelly cooed.

"How about you?" Coral asked.

Shelly scratched her head. "I'm not sure. Maybe my red sea-glass necklace?"

Coral grinned. "I've never seen anyone else with sea glass that color. I think that would be purr-fect!"

Angel frowned. "We can't just bring in seashells and sea glass!" she moaned. "We need something better!"

Coral and Shelly looked at each other. "Like what, Angel?" Coral asked.

"I don't know. But it has to be really different and special," Angel replied.

"What if we look around Leondra's Square today?" Shelly suggested. "We could each find something new."

"That's a great idea!" Coral agreed.

"No, it's not!" Angel cried. "Remember what Ms. Harbor said about curiosity? And about finding the most interesting things in the ocean?"

Her friends nodded.

"We aren't going to find anything amazing in Leondra's Square!" Angel continued. "We want things that the other purrmaids won't be able to find. We have to look somewhere no one else will think to look."

"But where are we supposed to go?" Shelly asked.

"I don't know," Angel replied.

"Let's have a snack," Coral said, "and we can think about it."

The girls swam into the kitchen. Mama had set out some of Coral's favorite sushi to share with her best friends. They floated around the counter and popped the sushi into their mouths with their paws.

"Don't let Mama see us," Coral said between bites. "She likes us to eat at the table."

Angel rolled her eyes. "Coral," she moaned.

"I'm sorry!" Coral sighed. "I don't like breaking the rules!"

Shelly and Angel laughed. They already knew that about their friend. Coral was definitely the most careful one in their group. Angel, on the other paw, wasn't much like her name at all. She loved to bend the rules. Shelly liked adventure, too—but not if it meant getting her paws dirty, and only when she didn't have to break *too* many rules.

Angel popped another piece of sushi into her mouth. Then her face lit up. "I have an idea!" she cried. "If we head out to the edges of Kittentail

Cove, there will be lots to discover. We can search Tortoiseshell Reef for something to bring to school!"

Coral gulped. Kittentail Cove was a big place, and Tortoiseshell Reef was as far away from home as they could go. Angel's plans were always exciting, but they were also complicated—and sometimes dangerous. From the way Angel was grinning, Coral knew that this plan would be no different.

"Maybe we should think about this some more," Coral began. "I mean . . . it might not be safe to go so far. There could be strong currents! And it's really close to where barracudas and giant squids and sharks hang out!"

"We'll stay away from the sharks, silly!" Angel answered. "You're paw-some at avoiding danger, right?"

Shelly agreed with Angel. But Coral shook her head and said, "I don't think this is a good idea."

"Okay! Okay!" Angel huffed. "If you don't want to try, we'll do something else."

Coral clenched her paws. "I do want to try!" she yowled. "I'm just afraid of what could happen. Haven't you ever been scared, Angel?"

Shelly swam between Coral and Angel. "You two shouldn't fight. We're best friends!" She turned to Angel and said, "It is a really great idea to search away from the center of Kittentail Cove. I bet Ms. Harbor would be really impressed by that. But Coral has a good point, too. Maybe we should think about this some more."

Shelly smiled, but Coral could see that she really wanted to go along with Angel's plan.

Then Angel said, "Well, if Coral's too much of a scaredy cat—"

"No! I can do this," Coral interrupted. She pictured Tortoiseshell Reef. She didn't know what was out there. But she was going to be brave, no matter how scary it was!

"Are you sure?" Shelly asked.

"Yes, I'm sure," Coral replied.

"Good," Angel said, "because meow is the time."

Ms. Harbor expected them to bring in something interesting tomorrow. Angel was right—it was meow or never.

"I'll race you to Tortoiseshell Reef!" Coral shouted. "Last one there is a rotten skeg!"

Coral zipped through the water. Angel and Shelly followed on her tail. In just a few minutes, they had passed Leondra's Square and were zooming toward Cove Council Hall. At first, Coral was purring with excitement. But the farther she got from home, the more butterfly fish fluttered in her tummy. What if something bad happened? What if there was a cat-tastrophe?

She tried to stop worrying. *I need to have a paw-sitive attitude,* she thought. *We're doing our homework. And then we're going straight home!*

As they reached Cove Council Hall, they saw Angel's mother, Mrs. Shore, speaking to Mayor Rivers. "Mommy!" Angel cried. She darted toward her mother to give her a hug. But she was going so fast that she spun Mrs. Shore around three times!

"Angel!" Mrs. Shore yelped. "Slow down!"

Mayor Rivers chuckled as he helped Mrs. Shore find her balance. "Angel, you've grown so big!" he said.

"And look at you two!" Mrs. Shore said to Coral and Shelly. She took their paws and gave them a squeeze. "How was the first day of school?"

"Purr-fect!" Coral replied. Angel and Shelly nodded in agreement.

"Our new teacher is Ms. Harbor," Shelly said.

"And she gave us a cool homework assignment!" Angel added. "We're supposed to bring something really special to class tomorrow."

"Is that why you're swimming so fast?" Mayor Rivers asked. "We have speed limits in this town, you know!"

Angel, Shelly, and Coral grinned. "We're going to Tortoiseshell Reef to see what interesting things we can find," Shelly said.

Mayor Rivers smiled. "I remember spending hours exploring Tortoiseshell Reef as a youth! If the reef is like it used to be, you will have lots of luck."

The girls giggled. Coral knew what her friends were thinking. Mayor Rivers was so *old*. Back in his youth, the reef must have been just a few elkhorns and sea fans!

"You know," Mrs. Shore said, "usually the most special things are the ones we hold close to our hearts."

"Does that mean we shouldn't go to Tortoiseshell Reef?" Coral asked.

"But, Mommy," Angel whined, "none of us have anything that is truly special at home! We have to go to Tortoiseshell Reef to search!" She clasped her paws and begged. "Please?"

"Just remember not to stay out too late," Mrs. Shore said. "It gets dark quicker at the edges of the cove. And the South Canary Current can get crowded in the evening." She pointed to the tall clock tower that topped Cove Council Hall. "You should all be home before dinner."

The South Canary Current flowed right past the entrance of Kittentail Cove. Most sea creatures used the current systems to get around the ocean quickly. When her parents took Coral to visit her cousins in other purrmaid towns, they used the South Canary Current. But Coral had forgotten that the current ran along the border of Tortoiseshell Reef.

"We'll be careful, Mrs. Shore," Shelly said.

"And we'll be back by dinnertime," Angel said.

"Good," Mrs. Shore replied. "I don't want you to run into any trouble on your adventure."

Coral gulped. That's what she was afraid of, too! But there was no way she was going to say so. She didn't want to be called a scaredy cat again.

"We won't, Mommy!" Angel agreed.

The three purrmaids swam off. Soon they arrived at Tortoiseshell Reef. They gazed around at the beautiful scenery.

"Don't you just love it here?" Shelly whispered.

Coral nodded. There were houses all over Kittentail Cove. Most purrmaids lived near Leondra's Square like Coral, Shelly, and Angel. Some lived farther out, especially the pearl farmers. There were many offices and restaurants near Cove Council Hall. Coral's father worked in one of those offices. So did Angel's mother. Shelly's parents had a restaurant there, too. But no one was allowed to build on Tortoiseshell Reef. The purrmaids of Kittentail Cove set it aside as a place to enjoy the ocean's natural beauty.

"I don't know why we don't come here more often," Angel said. She darted behind an elkhorn and disappeared.

"Angel?" Coral called. "Where are you?"

Angel popped up from behind a huge sea fan. "Here I am!" she shouted.

Coral yelped and hid behind Shelly.

"Coral!" Angel said. "You weren't scared, were you?"

"Of course I wasn't scared," Coral lied, "just surprised."

Shelly patted Coral's paw and said, "It's all right. Angel surprised me, too."

"I'm sorry," Angel apologized. She put her paw around Coral and led her toward the sea fan. "Can you help me with something?" she asked. When Coral nodded, Angel said, "I don't remember all the different creatures who live here in Tortoiseshell Reef. You know them better than I do. Will you show me?"

Coral smiled. Angel was a good friend. Together, they swam toward the floor of the reef. Coral pointed out different animals.

"That's a butterfly fish," Coral said. "And that is a cleaner shrimp."

"Cleaner than what?" Angel joked. The two purrmaids giggled.

"Look over here!" Shelly called. She was looking at something hiding inside a sea whip.

Coral swam closer to get a better look. She saw a beautiful orange-and-white fish zipping between the fronds of the sea whip. "It's a clown fish!" she whispered.

"Where's the rest of the circus?" Shelly laughed.

The clown fish didn't find the joke very funny. He swam away.

The purrmaids paddled slowly around the reef. Coral showed her friends all sorts of animals and plants. She spotted a family of sea horses. "Let's take a closer look," Coral suggested.

"Great idea!" Shelly agreed.

Coral looked over her shoulder. She started to wave to Angel. But Angel wasn't there!

Coral gasped. "Where is she?"

Shelly spun around. Coral knew she couldn't see Angel, either.

"Angel!" Coral yelled. "Where are you?" Her heart began to pound. *I knew something terrible would happen,* she thought.

Coral and Shelly kept shouting their friend's name. Finally, they reached the edge of Tortoiseshell Reef. The coral there had formed a deep tunnel. "Be careful near the tunnel," Coral warned Shelly. "Sometimes eels live in those!"

Suddenly, something came whooshing out of the tunnel. Without thinking, Coral swam in front of Shelly. She closed her eyes and braced herself for whatever was coming her way.

Then Coral heard giggling. She opened one eye. "Angel!" she yelped. "You scared me!"

"You scared me, too," Shelly added.

"We thought you were an eel!" Coral said. She was still trembling from fear.

"If you thought I was an eel," Angel said, "why did you swim in front of Shelly instead of swimming away?"

"I was—I was trying to protect her," Coral stammered.

Angel grinned. "You're not such a scaredy cat after all!"

Shelly gave Coral a hug. "That was pretty brave, Coral."

Coral smiled. "I guess it was," she said.

"Well, I have something else for you to be brave about," Angel said. She pointed to the tunnel. "It's the coolest thing. On the other side of the tunnel, there's a geyser that spins you head over tail. If you swim through really fast, it will flip you over and turn you around. Then you can swim back."

"That sounds so exciting!" Shelly said.

"Let's all do it!" Angel suggested.

"I—I don't know." Coral pulled back from her friends. "What if I can't do it and get stuck upside down? What if I sink? What if . . . ?" She hung her head in embarrassment.

"Haven't you ever tried a flip?" Angel asked. "I've been doing them since I was the size of a minnow!"

Coral felt as small as a grain of sand on the ocean floor. "No, I guess I haven't ever tried."

"We can help you," Angel offered.

"That's what friends do," Shelly added.

Coral sighed. "I don't think I could start by swimming the tunnel," she said.

"You don't have to!" Angel cried. She took Coral's paw. "Let's go over here." She led them to an open part of the ocean. "There's plenty of room to flip here!"

Coral gulped. "What do I do first?"

Shelly and Angel took turns showing Coral how to do underwater flips. "Look at me!" Angel yowled. She flipped easily, over and over again.

"The trick is to swim as fast as you can before you start the flip," Shelly said. She swam into the open water and did a flawless flip. "That way you have the oomph to get all the way around."

Coral narrowed her eyes. She shook her tail out to get loose. Then she started to swim.

Shelly said to go fast, so Coral swam with all her might. Then she tucked her head down and threw her tail back, just like Angel and Shelly had shown her.

And she did it!

Coral was catching her breath when Angel and Shelly swam up to her. "That was purr-fect!" Angel cried.

"You got it on the first try!" Shelly added.

Coral couldn't believe it! "That wasn't scary," she said.

"Do you want to try again?" Angel asked.

Coral nodded. "Yes, I do!"

The girls swam through the clear blue water. They took turns doing flips. Soon Coral couldn't remember why she had ever been afraid. "This is so much fun!" she shouted.

"I need a break!" Angel said. She plopped down on a rock. "I'm just going to sit here for a minute."

"Good idea," Shelly said. She sat down next to Angel.

Coral was tired, too. There was no room left on that rock, so she looked around for someplace else to rest.

That's when she realized nothing looked familiar. "Hey!" she shouted. "Do you know where we are? Because this is definitely not Kittentail Cove!"

"What do you mean, this isn't Kittentail Cove?" Angel asked.

"We're not allowed to leave the cove!" Shelly cried. "Where are we?"

"I don't know," Coral moaned. She bit her lip. "I wasn't paying attention while we were swimming and flipping."

"Neither was I," Shelly groaned.

Angel looked worried. "We're going to

be in so much trouble!" she said. "How are we going to get home?"

If there were little butterfly fish fluttering in Coral's tummy earlier, now it felt like big blue whales! She couldn't remember ever being this nervous. "We need to stay calm!" she said. "We just need to look around. I'm sure we'll see something familiar soon. And then we'll hurry home!"

"Good plan," Shelly agreed. "Should we split up? That way we can see more of the ocean at once."

Angel shook her head. "I don't want to be alone out here! I think it's better for us to stay together."

For once, Coral agreed with Angel's plan. She nodded and said, "Come on. Let's try to retrace our swim."

The three purrmaids moved slowly through the water. They couldn't see Tortoiseshell Reef from where they were. All there was up ahead was a giant kelp forest.

Every moment they were lost made Coral worry more. *What are we going to do?* she thought.

Coral, Shelly, and Angel were very busy trying to find their way home. So they didn't notice the school of fish swimming toward them until they were surrounded by a hundred bright-green parrot fish.

Suddenly, Coral remembered something. "The South Canary Current!" she shouted. "Maybe these fish are headed there!"

Shelly's face lit up. "If we can find the South Canary Current . . ."

". . . it will take us home to Kittentail Cove!" Coral finished.

"You are so smart!" Angel applauded. "I knew there was nothing to worry about!"

Coral rolled her eyes. Angel had *definitely* been worried! "Let's follow those fish," she said.

There were so many parrot fish, they formed a green cloud. That made it easy to follow them without spooking them. Soon Shelly cried, "Look over there! It's the South Canary Current!"

A line of fish, turtles, and other sea creatures traveled in the flow of the South

Canary Current. It was like a high-speed highway for ocean folks. "We'll be home in no time!" Coral cheered. She started to swim toward the current.

But Angel grabbed Coral's paw. "Don't!" she yelled.

"Why?" Coral asked. "We have to go!"

Angel wouldn't let go. She pointed at the water in front of them. "Does that look like smooth sailing to you?"

Coral scowled. "I don't understand."

"Look closely," Angel urged.

"Is that a swarm of jellyfish up ahead?" Shelly gasped.

"I think it is," Angel said. Jellyfish were pretty harmless to purrmaids—unless they got stuck in a big group of them. One sting wasn't so bad, but getting stung over and over was not a good idea. "We can't go straight to the current."

"We have to find a way to go around them," Coral agreed.

"But they're everywhere," Shelly said. She was right. As the girls swam closer, they saw that the cloud of jellyfish stretched over most of the ocean. It was in front of them, from the top of the kelp forest almost to the surface of the water.

Angel pointed downward at the kelp forest. "If we can't go up, we'll go down."

Shelly shrugged. Coral frowned. But then they both nodded.

"I'll go first," Angel said. She swam toward the kelp. Shelly followed on her tail.

Coral hesitated. She was trying to be brave in front of her friends. But she felt nervous. *Who knew what was hiding in all that kelp?*

"Come on, Coral!" Shelly said.

"It's not so bad," Angel added. "Don't be a scaredy cat!"

Coral lowered her eyes. She didn't mean to be scared. She just liked doing things the safe way. The safe way never involved sharks or jellyfish or getting grounded. But now the safe way seemed to be through the forest. She gulped, then shouted, "I'm coming!"

The three friends entered the kelp forest together. There were a few natural passages that let them swim freely. But in other parts of the forest, the girls had to use their paws to part the kelp in order to get through.

"How do we know if we're going the right way?" Shelly asked.

Coral looked up. She tried to catch a glimpse of the South Canary Current, but all she could see was kelp. "I don't know," she answered.

"Let's keep moving," Angel suggested.

Coral nodded. She pushed aside a large kelp leaf. "Wow!" she cried.

"What is it?" Shelly asked. She shrank behind Angel. "Is it dangerous?"

Coral grinned. "No! It's the way out!" She held the kelp aside so her friends could swim through. They were back in the open ocean!

"Where's the current?" Angel looked around.

"It's up there!" Shelly said. "And I don't see any jellyfish, either!"

"Let's go!" Angel cried.

But Coral didn't move. She was staring at a trench in front of them. When she looked down, the water was darkened by shadows.

Coral thought something was lodged in the sand at the bottom of the trench. At first, it looked like a whale resting on the ocean floor. But then she realized it wasn't a living creature. "We've found a shipwreck!"

"I can't believe it!" Coral whispered. "I've read about shipwrecks. But I've never seen one!"

"That's because you never leave Kittentail Cove," Angel purred.

Coral scowled at Angel. But when she saw Angel's face, she knew her friend was kidding.

"Speaking of Kittentail Cove," Shelly said, "it's time for us to get back."

"I want to tell everyone at home about what we found!" Angel said.

"Wait!" Coral shouted. She gazed down at the shadowy ship. All afternoon, every time she had gotten scared, she had made herself be brave. If she could do it one more time, she and her friends could find something truly paw-some. "We have to explore the shipwreck first!"

Shelly's eyes grew wide, and Angel's jaw looked like it was going to fall off. "What did you say?" Angel sputtered.

"The South Canary Current will get us home in a flash," Coral said. "So I think we have a little bit of time. Just a quick look won't hurt, right?" She smiled. "Maybe we'll find something in the shipwreck to bring to school."

"That would be fin-tastic!" Angel said. She shrugged. "I guess I'm in!"

"Me too," Shelly said. "We won't get a chance like this again."

Coral started to swim down into the trench. Angel and Shelly swam beside her. "We can't explore for too long," she said.

"There's the Coral we know and love!" Shelly laughed.

"I'm serious!" Coral added. "We have to be home soon. I don't want to—"

"Get grounded," Angel said. "We know, we know."

Shelly elbowed Coral playfully. "We'll just take a quick peek." She flipped in the water, grinning. "This is so cool!"

The purrmaids swam closer to the ship. It had sunk down into the sand and was tipped over to one side. Giant barnacles covered the hull. Tattered bits of sail hung from the masts. There were holes scattered

around the deck. Beams of sunlight shone down to light different parts of the ship.

Coral peeked in a jagged hole to see into the ship's hold. A small fish swam out toward her. The hold was too dark to see very far. "This is scarier up close," she whispered.

"Do you want to go inside?" Angel asked.

Coral gulped. She didn't know if she could be brave enough to do that. But then she noticed a fancy door. It didn't look as creepy as the hold. She pointed. "Let's look there instead," she suggested.

All three girls had to yank on the handle to get it open.

"I hope this is worth it," Angel muttered.

Shelly peered through the door. "It's worth it!" she shouted, and raced ahead.

The room behind the door must have belonged to the captain of the ship. The floor and the walls were dotted with holes just like on the deck outside. Shelly swam straight to a large table nailed to the floor in the middle of the room. Angel studied the giant globe on one side of the room. Coral saw that the floor was littered with barrels, coils of rope, and tangles of seaweed. She took the lid off one of the barrels.

Something popped out and Coral squealed. "Yikes!"

Immediately, Angel and Shelly came to her side. "What happened?" Angel asked.

"That little guy scared me!" Coral said. A small crab scuttled away.

The girls giggled. Then Shelly said, "Come over here!" She led her friends back to the table. "Look what I found!" She held up a small golden tube. When she pulled on one end of the tube, it extended to be longer than Shelly's whole arm.

"What is it?" Angel asked.

"I think it's a spyglass," Shelly said.

Coral nodded. "Human sailors use these to see things far away," she said.

"I've never actually seen one," Shelly said.

"So it's purr-fect to show Ms. Harbor!" Angel grinned from ear to ear.

"One down, two to go!" Coral laughed. She put one paw around Angel's waist and the other around Shelly's. She hugged them tightly. "Let's see what else we can find!"

Angel's face lit up. "Actually, I have something to show you, too." She swam back to the globe.

Coral frowned. "Hey, Angel, you know that is way too heavy for us to carry home, right? Even if it wasn't nailed to the floor!"

"I know, Coral." Angel laughed. "I wasn't talking about the globe. I wanted to show you this." She held out her paw.

Coral swam closer to examine a small silver circle. She noticed a tiny needle under a glass cover, pointing at the letter N. "You found a compass!" she cried.

"It still works, too!" Angel turned around and waved the compass. She held it out again. The needle spun and pointed to N for north.

"It's paw-some, Angel," Shelly said.

"I'm bringing this to school tomorrow,"

Angel said. "That spyglass and this compass are purr-fect treasures from a shipwreck!"

Coral smiled, but she didn't feel completely happy. *Angel and Shelly found fabulous treasures to share with Ms. Harbor tomorrow, she* thought. *But I still have nothing. And it was* my *idea to come here in the first place. It's not fair!*

Shelly had the same thought. "Angel and I have our special things," she said. "We just need to find something for you, Coral."

Coral nodded. But there was nothing else in the captain's room that she could bring to school. Then she had an idea. "We still have the hold to search!" she cried. She pointed to a hole in the floor. "We can get down through here."

"I thought you said it was scary in there," Angel said.

Coral shrugged. "You keep saying not to be a scaredy cat. And we've been fine so far." She darted through the hole in the floor. "See if you two can keep up with me!"

7

The floor of the hold was covered in sand, sea-weed, and coral. It was like being in an under-water cave instead of a human ship. There were broken barrels scattered on the ground. Some sunlight filtered down from above.

Coral ignored all of that. She swam right to a half-open chest that was lit by a single sunbeam. "Over here!" she shouted.

"Wow!" Angel gasped. "Look at all these coins!"

Coral picked one up. "They're beautiful!" Purrmaids sometimes found one or two human coins around the ocean. But the girls had never seen this many in one place. "I'm going to bring a gold coin to school tomorrow!" she announced.

"That's a great idea!" Angel said.

Coral's cheeks hurt from grinning. *I'm so glad I was brave!* she thought. She squeezed the coin in her paw and said, "Let's get back to the South Canary Current. It's time to go home!"

The girls closed the lid of the chest and turned around to leave. Suddenly, the sunlight disappeared. "What happened to the sun?" Shelly asked.

Coral looked up. There was nothing blocking the holes in the deck. "It must have gotten cloudy," she answered.

"It's really dark now," Angel said. "I can't even see my tail!"

Coral scanned the darkened water. She pointed to a brighter spot in the darkness. "I think that's the hole we used to get down here. Let's head that way and see if we can get out."

The purrmaids dodged corals and sea sponges as they swam slowly toward the light. But Coral realized they weren't swimming toward sunlight. Sunlight wasn't green, and this light definitely was. This was more of a glow than a ray of light.

There were many harmless creatures in the ocean that glowed. Sea pens, krill, and lantern fish could all glow. Coral didn't think this was any of those things. None of them had sharp, scary teeth. But this thing did!

Coral hissed. "Quick! Hide!" She grabbed her friends' paws and pulled them behind a barrel. When they were hidden, she carefully peeked out to get a better look at the glowing creature.

The eerie green glow circled around the hold. It paused near the barrel. Now it was close enough for Coral to see its eyes.

"It looks like a monster!" Shelly whispered.

Coral bit her lip. "I think it's a shark," she said.

"A shark!" Angel gasped. "I knew we should have just gone home!"

Coral scowled. Angel was probably right. But they couldn't change that now. They had to think of some way to escape.

The trio huddled together. "The next time he moves away," Coral said, "we should swim as fast as we can!"

Shelly and Angel nodded. They watched the ghostly glow pass back and forth through the murky waters. Then it began to head toward the barrel. "What is he doing?" Angel gasped.

Coral panicked. *This is all my fault,* she thought. *We never should have come down to the hold.*

The shark paused at a giant sea fan. The glow from his skin cast creepy shadows on the ocean floor. That's when Coral saw her chance.

"Go, go, go!" she hissed.

Angel and Shelly raced away. Coral didn't follow them.

She knew they couldn't all outswim the shark. To make sure her friends were safe, Coral had to create a distraction.

She knew what she had to do.

Coral squared her shoulders. She popped up from behind the barrel and swam straight at the shark. When she got close, she tucked her head down and threw her tail back. Hopefully, the bubbles from her underwater flip would get the shark's attention.

It worked. He tilted his head toward her.

Shelly and Angel had reached a hole in the hold's wall. They just needed a little more time to get to safety. So Coral let go of her coin and waved her paws around while shouting, "Over here, Mr. Shark! Eat me if you want! But stay away from my friends!"

The green-glowing shark swam slowly in Coral's direction. She felt herself trembling.

But she had to be strong. She forced herself to look directly at the shark.

When they were eye to eye, though, Coral's courage faded away. She gulped.

The shark said, "Eat you? Why would I want to eat you?"

8

"You're—you're not here to eat me?" Coral stammered.

"Of course not!" the shark snapped.

"But you're a shark. That's what you do." Coral scratched her head. "Isn't it?"

"Catsharks always get a bad rap," he grumbled. "Everyone in the ocean thinks we're out to eat them!" He gestured at a stack of pale yellow pouches that hung from the sea fan. "I'm stuck here baby-sitting. These are my cousins. My mom and my aunt went to get a bite to eat."

Coral's eyes grew wide. The shark saw that she was scared, so he shouted, "Worms! We eat worms! Or tiny fish! Or shrimp!"

Coral exhaled with relief. "I didn't know you weren't a purrmaid-eating type of shark," she admitted.

"Well, you're not the only one." The shark sighed. "Why do you think we live inside a shipwreck? Nobody wants us around. Everyone says we're too danger-ous." He swam back to the sea fan. "No one even bothers to get to know us."

Coral felt awful. She didn't know any-thing about catsharks.

She swam to his side. "I'm Coral," she said. "I'm a purrmaid from Kittentail Cove."

"I'm Chomp," he answered. "I'm from right here."

Coral giggled. "It's nice to meet you, Chomp."

"What are you doing down here inside the shipwreck?" Chomp asked. "And the two purrmaids who swam away—were those your friends?"

Coral nodded. "My best friends, actually. We were trying to find the South Canary Current. Then we saw the shipwreck, and we wanted to explore."

"It's a pretty cool place to live," Chomp said.

"It really is!" Coral agreed. "But it's time for us to get home."

Shelly said. "When we got out and you weren't here . . . we didn't know what to do!"

"We were so scared!" Angel added.

"I didn't mean to scare you," Coral said. "I wanted to give you more time to get away. But I didn't need to do that!"

"What happened with the monster?" Shelly asked.

"He isn't a monster!" Coral explained.

"Come and visit again sometime," Chomp said.

"And you should come visit me, too!" Coral suggested. "All you have to do is ride the South Canary Current. It will bring you directly to the entrance of Kittentail Cove."

"I'll remember that!" Chomp answered. He waved goodbye.

By the time Coral swam out of the shipwreck, she was grinning from ear to ear. It had been an exciting day!

Then Angel's voice startled her. "Coral! You're alive!"

Shelly and Angel hurried over to their friend's side. "We thought you were right behind us,"

"He's a catshark, and catsharks don't eat purrmaids."

"What a relief!" Shelly said.

"I think there's been enough adventure today," Angel purred. "Let's get to the current so we can go home."

The purrmaids hurried up to the South Canary Current. It was as crowded as Angel's mother had warned it would be.

From time to time, they got bumped by turtles, fish, and even other purrmaids. The girls stayed close together and kept an eye on each other.

When they took the exit to Kittentail Cove and swam through the gates of the town, Coral glanced up at the clock tower. "We made it!" she cried. "It isn't dinnertime yet!"

"That means we won't get grounded," Angel laughed, "*and* we found the coolest treasures to bring to school tomorrow!"

Coral froze. Her gold coin! "Oh no!" she moaned. "I don't have my treasure!"

"What do you mean?" Shelly asked.

"I must have dropped my coin at the shipwreck!" Coral said. "When I was trying to get Chomp's attention, I started waving my paws around." She looked down at her tail. "I think I let go of it then."

Angel and Shelly glanced at each other.

"You can have my treasure," Shelly offered.

"Or mine," Angel added.

Coral shook her head. "It's really nice of you to say that," she said. "But I can't take your stuff! That wouldn't be fair." She sighed. "It's my fault I lost the coin. I'll just bring in that shell from my collection."

Coral tried to cheer up as they swam home. But when they reached Leondra's Square, she was still feeling down. Her friends each gave her a hug when they said goodbye, but even that didn't help.

"We'll see you here tomorrow?" Angel asked.

Coral nodded. "Of course."

"Smile, Coral," Shelly said. "Things will be better tomorrow, I'm sure."

Coral tried to smile for Shelly. But in her heart, she was thinking, *They couldn't get any worse.*

Coral hardly slept that night. She tossed and turned on her oyster-shell bed for hours.

She knew she was running behind because she was moving so slowly. But when she got to Leondra's Square to meet up with Angel and Shelly, she realized how late she was. Not only was Shelly already waiting, but Angel was there, too!

"Sorry I'm a little slow today," Coral said.

"Don't worry!" Angel answered. Shelly and Angel exchanged a glance. They had huge grins on their faces.

"Let's get to school," Shelly suggested. "We have our treasures now!"

Coral bit her lip. It was nice to see Angel and Shelly so excited about the treasures they found in the shipwreck. It wasn't their fault that Coral had lost hers. She forced herself to smile and swam alongside her friends.

As the students arrived in Eel-Twelve, Ms. Harbor welcomed them. "I hope you all brought something to share," she said. The students nodded. Ms. Harbor smiled. "I can't wait to see your treasures and begin getting to know all of you."

"Can I go first?" Baker asked.

"No, me!" Taylor shouted.

"Everyone will get a turn, I purr-omise," Ms. Harbor said.

Ms. Harbor called up one purrmaid at a time to present a treasure. Coral did her best to pay attention, but she kept thinking about the gold coin. *I can't believe I lost it,* she thought. *It would have been so purr-fect for today!*

Coral didn't notice it was Angel's turn until Shelly tapped her shoulder. She looked up and saw that Angel was floating in the front of the classroom.

"Shelly and I will present together," Angel announced. She winked at Coral.

Of course they're presenting as a team, Coral thought. *The spyglass and compass go together.*

Shelly tugged on Coral's paw. "Come on, Coral," she said.

Coral shook her head. "I don't have my

coin," she whispered. "My treasure doesn't
match yours!"

"You're wrong!" Shelly said. She dragged
Coral to float next to Angel.

"There are many things in the ocean that
are special to Shelly and me," Angel said.
"But nothing is more special than family
and friends."

"We're both really lucky to have fin-tastic families," Shelly continued. "But the treasure Angel and I want to share today is our best friend, Coral."

All eyes turned to Coral. She didn't under-stand what was going on. Angel didn't give her a chance to ask any questions. "Yester-day, we learned that the most special things in the world are the ones we hold close to our hearts," Angel said.

"Sometimes Coral can be extra careful," Shelly continued, "and that can make some purrmaids think she's a scaredy cat."

"But she's not!" Angel said. "She's actu-ally one of the bravest purrmaids I know."

"She's only cautious because she cares so much about her friends," Shelly added. "Coral would do anything for us, and we would do anything for her."

"There is nothing closer to our hearts

than our best friend," Angel said.

"What a wonderful presentation!" Ms. Harbor cried. "Well done, Shelly and Angel!"

Coral could feel her face getting hot. "I treasure you two, as well," she said, and the whole class cheered.

Coral was very quiet as she swam out to recess. She was speechless after Shelly and Angel's presentation. They had made her feel so loved and special. She couldn't believe how lucky she was to have such good friends.

Angel and Shelly weren't sure why Coral was so quiet. "Did we do something wrong?" Shelly asked.

"We were trying to be nice," Angel added.

"No, no, no!" Coral cried. She rushed forward to hug her friends. "That was one of the nicest things anyone has ever done for me!"

Shelly and Angel beamed. But the moment was interrupted when the girls heard their classmate Taylor scream, "A shark!"

"He's coming for us!" Baker shouted. "Swim for your lives!"

Coral whipped around to see what was happening. That's when she saw someone familiar.

The other purrmaids cowered behind the rock benches in the schoolyard. Ms. Harbor swam toward the shark, ready to protect her students. Coral darted forward and put herself between the shark and Ms. Harbor. "Chomp!" she shouted. "What are you doing here?"

Chomp grinned, and all of his teeth were on display. That caused a new chorus of screams from Coral's classmates.

"Get away, Coral! He'll eat you!" Taylor yelled.

Coral turned around and shook her head. "No, he won't," she replied. She motioned for the purrmaids to stop hiding. Angel and Shelly gulped, but they swam out from behind the benches. The rest of her classmates poked their heads out but didn't come forward.

Coral said, "Ms. Harbor, I'd like to introduce you to someone—my new friend, Chomp."

Ms. Harbor opened and closed her mouth like a fish. But she didn't make a sound. Chomp gave her a toothy grin and extended his fin. Coral nodded at her teacher. Ms. Harbor finally put her paw out so they could shake.

"Chomp is a catshark," Coral continued, "and yesterday, I learned a lot." She winked at Shelly and Angel. "My best friends helped me learn that I don't have to be a scaredy cat about new things." She smiled at Chomp. "And Chomp taught me that catsharks aren't dangerous. They are just misunderstood."

"Really?" Baker asked.

"Really," Chomp answered. "I didn't come to Kittentail Cove for lunch! I came to give this to Coral." He held out a small package wrapped in seaweed.

"What is that?" Ms. Harbor asked.

Chomp grinned again. "Coral isn't the only one who learned something," he explained. "She taught me there are other good fish in the sea. You just have to be willing to give them a chance, and maybe you'll make a new friend."

Coral unwrapped the package. Inside were three gold coins from the shipwreck!

"After you left," Chomp said, "I realized you dropped your coin. I wanted to bring it to you so you'd always remember me." He giggled. "I brought some extras—for your two friends. And I added some hooks so you can attach them to your bracelets. That way you won't lose them!"

Once again, Coral was speechless.

"How fin-tastic!" Ms. Harbor cheered. "Thank you both for teaching us about catsharks. And thank you for visiting, Chomp, and for introducing him, Coral. What a purr-fect thing to share with the class—a new friend!"

The entire class cheered. Coral gave Chomp a big hug. The other purrmaids swam up to him and started asking questions. Coral pulled Angel and Shelly aside. She held out a gold coin to each of them.

"But Chomp gave those to you!" Angel said.

Coral shook her head. "He wanted us each to have a coin. We can put them on our bracelets to remind us to be brave."

"That is a paw-some plan!" Shelly cried.

Coral put her gold coin on her bracelet.
She smiled and purred, "I can't wait for our
next adventure!"

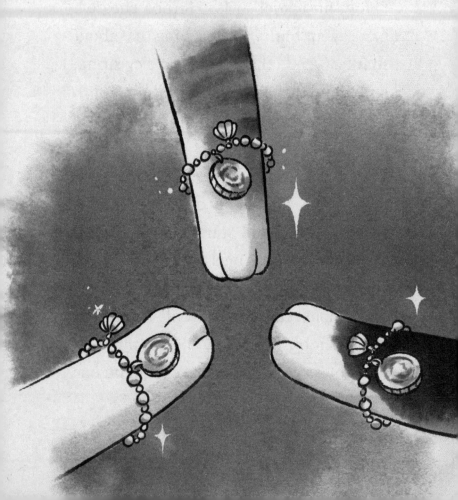

Don't miss
the next adventure!

Excerpt copyright © 2017 by Sudipta Bardhan-Quallen.
Interior illustrations © 2017 by Vivien Wu.
Published in the United States by Random House Children's Books,
a division of Penguin Random House LLC, New York.

Normally, when Angel was that excited, it was hard for her to sit still and listen. But not while Ms. Harbor talked about all her favorite artists! When the bell rang, she was disappointed that the day was over!

Right after school, the girls headed to Cove Council Hall. Shelly and Coral struggled to keep up with Angel.

"Slow down, Angel!" Coral begged.

"Why are you speeding?" Shelly panted.

"The tour!" Angel replied. "I want to be the first ones to see the museum after the grand makeover!"

Everyone knew Angel loved being first. Winning, getting prizes, and being the best were all things that Angel tried hard to do. But getting to the museum today wasn't just about winning. She thought they could get some good ideas about their homework from the museum.

Angel practically dragged Mommy out of her office. But when the four of them reached the front door of the museum, it was locked! Mommy looked at her watch. "The tour doesn't start for fifteen minutes," she explained. "We will have to wait."

"Rats!" Angel grumbled. All she wanted to do was to go inside.

"Let's get in line," Shelly suggested, "so we can be the first ones in."

"Great idea!" Angel agreed.

The girls lined up right in front of the museum. Slowly, other purrmaids gathered around the door, too. But the tour couldn't start without Mayor Rivers. "Where is the mayor?" Angel wondered, straining to see over the crowd of purrmaids.

Finally, she spied him. "We're going to be able to go in soon!" Angel squealed. She grabbed her friends' paws and danced around with happiness.

Mayor Rivers stopped near Mommy, and Angel's heart sank. He always talked for so long! Now they would have to wait again.

As she frowned at the talkative mayor, Angel didn't notice anyone swimming past. But then Shelly yowled, "Hey! You can't cut in front of us!"

It was the Catfish Club!